TINY'S
BATH

For M. and D.
—C. M.

To my ninety-five-year-old grandmother,
Gaga, who showed me how to love laughter,
a good story, and God. I love you.
—R. D.

PUFFIN BOOKS
Published by the Penguin Group
Penguin Putnam Inc., 375 Hudson Street, New York, New York 10014, U.S.A.
Penguin Books Ltd, 27 Wrights Lane, London W8 5TZ, England
Penguin Books Australia Ltd, Ringwood, Victoria, Australia
Penguin Books Canada Ltd, 10 Alcorn Avenue, Toronto, Ontario, Canada M4V 3B2
Penguin Books (N.Z.) Ltd, 182-190 Wairau Road, Auckland 10, New Zealand

Penguin Books Ltd, Registered Offices: Harmondsworth, Middlesex, England

First published by Puffin Books and Viking, members of Penguin Putnam Books for
Young Readers, 1998

1 3 5 7 9 10 8 6 4 2

Text copyright © Cari Meister, 1998
Illustrations copyright © Rich Davis, 1998
All rights reserved

LIBRARY OF CONGRESS CATALOGING-IN-PUBLICATION DATA
Meister, Cari.
Tiny's bath / by Cari Meister ; illustrated by Rich Davis.   p. cm.
Summary: Tiny is a very big dog who loves to dig, and when it is time for his bath,
his owner has trouble finding a place to bathe him.
ISBN 0-670-87962-2 (Viking : hc).—ISBN 0-14-130267-4 (Puffin : pb)
[1. Dogs—Fiction. 2. Baths—Fiction.] I. Davis, Rich, date, ill. II. Title.
PZ7.M515916Ti 1998 [E]—dc21 98-3844 CIP AC
Printed in Hong Kong
Puffin® and Easy-to-Read® are registered trademarks of Penguin Putnam Inc.

Reading level 1.3

TINY'S
BATH

by Cari Meister
illustrated by Rich Davis

PUFFIN BOOKS

I have a very large dog.

His name is Tiny.

He is bigger than a bike.

He is bigger than a chair.

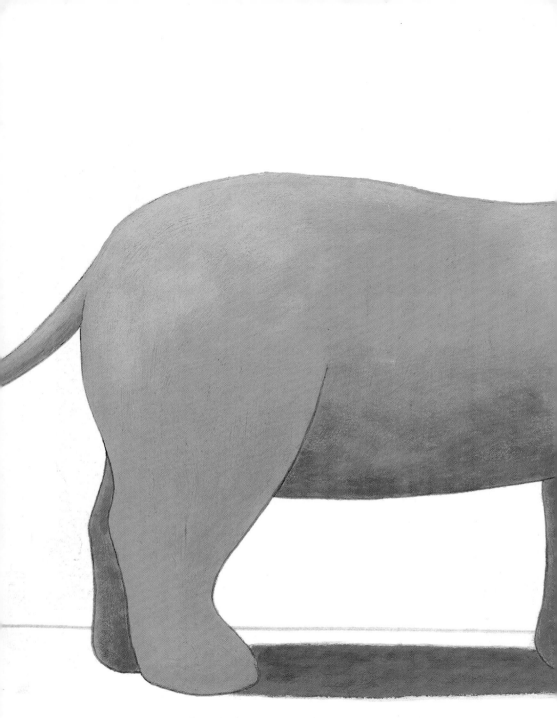

He is bigger than I am!

Tiny likes to dig.

He is dirty.

He needs a bath.

The pail is too small.

The sink is too small.

The bathtub is too small.

Where can I give Tiny a bath?

My pool!

Get the hose.

Get the brush. Get the soap.

Scrub, scrub, scrub.

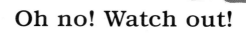

Oh no! Watch out!

Tiny is clean. I am wet.

Stop, Tiny! Come back!

Oh no! Mud!

Tiny is dirty.

I am dirty.

Back to the pool.